Raffi Songs to Read®
FIVE LITTLE DUCKS
Illustrated by Jose Aruego and Ariane Dewey

⬛Harcourt

Orlando Boston Dallas Chicago San Diego

Visit *The Learning Site!*
www.harcourtschool.com

This edition is published by special arrangement with Random House Children's Books, a division of Random House, Inc.

Grateful acknowledgment is made to Random House Children's Books, a division of Random House, Inc.
for permission to reprint *Five Little Ducks* by Raffi, illustrated by Jose Aruego and Ariane Dewey.
Text copyright © 1989 by Troubadour Learning, a division of Troubadour Records Ltd.;
illustrations copyright © 1989 by Jose Aruego and Ariane Dewey.

Printed in the United States of America

ISBN 0-15-315201-X

15 16 17 18 19 20 060 09 08 07 06 05 04

Five little ducks went out one day,
Over the hills and far away.

Mother Duck said,
"Quack, quack, quack, quack."

But only four little ducks came back.

Four little ducks went out one day,
Over the hills and far away.

Mother Duck said,
"Quack, quack, quack, quack."

But only three little ducks came back.

Three little ducks went out one day,
Over the hills and far away.

Mother Duck said,
"Quack, quack, quack, quack."

But only two little ducks came back.

Two little ducks went out one day,
Over the hills and far away.

Mother Duck said,
"Quack, quack, quack, quack."

But only one little duck came back.

One little duck went out one day,
Over the hills and far away.

Mother Duck said,
"Quack, quack, quack, quack."

But none of the five little ducks came back.

Sad Mother Duck went out one day,
Over the hills and far away.

Mother Duck said, "Quack, quack, quack, quack!"

And all of the five little ducks came back.

FIVE LITTLE DUCKS

Brightly

Five lit-tle ducks went out one day, O- ver the hills and far a- way. Mo- ther duck said. "Quack, quack, quack, quack!" But on- ly four lit- tle ducks came back.

2. Four little ducks went out one day...
   But only three little ducks came back.

3. Three little ducks went out one day...
   But only two little ducks came back.

4. Two little ducks went out one day...
   But only one little duck came back.

5. One little duck went out one day...
   But none of the five little ducks came back.

6. Sad mother duck went out one day...
   And all of the five little ducks came back.